EXPLOSIVE PASSION

EXPLOSIVE PASSION

Love Poems and Short Stories

Nader Somoye

EXPLOSIVE PASSION
LOVE POEMS AND SHORT STORIES

iUniverse books may be ordered through booksellers or by contacting:

iUniverse
1663 Liberty Drive
Bloomington, IN 47403
www.iuniverse.com
1-800-Authors (1-800-288-4677)

Because of the dynamic nature of the internet, any web addresses or links contained in this book may have changed since publication and may no longer be valid. The views expressed in this work are solely those of the author and do not necessarily reflect the views of the publisher, and the publisher hereby disclaims any responsibility for them.

Any people depicted in stock imagery provided by Getty Images are models, and such images are being used for illustrative purposes only. Certain stock imagery © Getty Images.

ISBN: 978-1-5320-6657-3 (sc)
ISBN: 978-1-5320-6656-6 (e)

Library of Congress Control Number: 2019900469

Print information available on the last page.

iUniverse rev. date: 02/14/2019

A rich selection of powerful poems of
passion and intense short stories

Contents

The Hunger Within

Waking up in this glorious rising sunshine of another unpredictable day. Seeing the magnificent globe-like reflection through my dainty-looking half-open derelict window, in need of repairs. Feeling the cool, rejuvenating breeze, seeping pertinaciously over scented flowery layered windowsill, filling my not-so-quite-awake mind with sweet aroma. Bathing the softness of my almost naked, sensual chocolate-colored body, portraying a perfectly formed work of art. Lying motionless on my one-thousand-thread-count snowy-white Egyptian cotton sheet, which never fails to lead me into the comfort of the clouds above. Leaving me yearning to be touched. To be loved. With this mysterious glowing sunshine. Creating havoc on my womanhood. Its razor-sharp glow taunting the hardness of my rising nipples. Penetrating my bedeviled body to a fiery level. Releasing a robust comfort of need. Giving birth to a strange, anxious sensation wanting to be coddled. Sending vicious cries bursting from my nervous lips. Shaky fingers playing sweet music on my gracious moist, hairy arena. Slowly flickering into an inner need of excitable satisfaction. Wetness now springing from my overwhelming fountain of love. As the music of celebration continues and my body heightens with emotion, the springy evolution within me pouring more and more. Increasing my desire onto a platform of great heights. Taking me into the world beyond. Finally, out of control, shaking with hunger, unable to contain myself. My legs parted, waiting to receive my blessing. Screams suddenly bursting deep within as an unknown soul takes over my body, conjugating in harmony.

Blissful it was. My body finally slowing down to a dynamic calm. From extrasensory emotions to total satisfaction. Descending back to earth with such solemn peace within my soul. Hunger and desire fulfills, a dream truly experienced.

The Missing Link

Loneliness leaves a void deep, deep within. An emptiness so indescribable, no words can define it. So bent out of shape and proportioned, it feels like a desert as far as the eyes can see, until tears flow like a river. Bareness, sadness, isolation, and depression. Like a blank canvas that looks ready to capture. A body standing alone, unsheltered, enslaved, but one that can be evolved. A stomach filled only with echoes. A soul in need of a soul mate that can satisfy your needs. Needy bodies wanting to ignite with that fiery sensation. Finally, closure through the art of lovemaking that makes one's heart desire more. Enkindling one's emotion. The emptiness replaced with joy and fulfillment. Blood now flows profusely through narcotic veins, empowering the body and the soul, rejuvenating the motion once more toward an enfranchising life. Satisfaction of equanimity grows to the peak until emptiness is no more.

Inner Thoughts

Sitting in St. Peter's Cemetery on that bright Sunday morning, a place no other wanted to be but me. The chairs were ragged and broken but strong enough to accommodate my voluptuous being. The sun reflects off my worried, aging face, with questionable thoughts. Preparing for the invasion of my virgin pasture.

Sitting among the long-forgotten and the newly forgotten. Little people, big people, mighty people, and not-so-mighty people. It brings mental pain, crippling pain, confusion to head and body. Physical pain entraps the inner me, pinning my feet to the earth, leaving my whole being motionless. I wonder what it would be like if they all had a second chance at life. Would they be sad, happy, or indifferent? Would there be joy in their lives? I wonder, *How will I end up?* If only one knew. Time waits for no man. Sitting in this atmosphere of peace and tranquility has left me with the desire to move forward, to make a difference in my life, a fulfilled life.

If only I knew how.

The Stallion

So long have I waited for this majestic moment. So long as the burning desire crippled my voluptuous and wanting body. So long as magnificent sensations roamed within me, no outlet to be found. Now the moment is near, as this rugged, perfectly formed body lies next to me. Kissing the hardness of his lustrous lips, heavy with need, my fingers combing through his dark jungle-curly hair, feeling like silk, kissing his crispy ears of wonder, touching his G-spot and hearing his moans and fighting back the never-ending tears of pleasure. Softly, under his breath, he mutters sweet words of passion. Moving my hand gingerly along his well-aligned body. Slowly sweeping over his broad, hairy, muscular chest, so defined you can feel his heartbeat. Listening to his throbbing heartbeat, sending vibrations through my already numbed body, playing stimulating sweet music to my eager ears. Slowly moving my nervous, excited fingers to the main attraction, his hardened hairy playground. Wow, it is huge. Excitement captivates my mind and my already sensual body as I explore what will soon be mine. It seems motionless, waiting for my fingers to activate it, like a lethal snake hovering in the grass, patiently awaiting its prey. Soon, too soon, there is a rigid hardness. Excitement fills my stomach as I slowly stroke this magnificent stallion of a man. It is a beast in its own right, a weapon so strong and powerful within my palm, giving pulsations that my heart's desire is about to bring forth truth. My long wait will soon no longer be, as this precious weapon heightens upward in an exuberant receiving position. With its vein shouting out, so ridged, my heart skips a beat for a moment, breathlessly. I straddle, widening my shaky but anxious legs across this beautiful wanting beast, allowing it to feel my wetness, to play with its prey in the grassy meadow of my almost virgin pool of moisture. Slowly, with a small, excited scream, escaping almost breathlessly, I allow a grand entry as I give praises to my god in the clouds. No words can express this awesome penetration as the beast enters and conquers this long-awaiting, taunting desire. Slowly I ride into the unknown outer world, experienced only when vibrant bodies truly become one.

Receiving the long-awaited deep, robust pumping within me, I continue to ride this great monster of pleasure. Sweet sweat showers my body as it gets deeper and deeper, sending shouts of joyous satisfaction from my lips, with tears of celebration rolling down my cheeks. I continue to contract, injecting my juices into the beast, making him slippery, forcing him into a robust state, working him harder to keep up with me. Suddenly, there are simultaneous cries from both of us as we finally reach our exuberant, exhausting peak, but we continue to hold on for our lives, neither wanting this great experience to rupture. Yes, yes, I thank the universe for this moment in time!

Romeo and Juliet: The Endless Love

A love so powerful, it sends shocking volts of electric current throughout my starved being. Bodies, from their toes to their untuned minds, blessed and sanctified by the Gods of love of all men. An endless love so entranced and perfectly formed, it makes me feel like heaven on earth, like a wedding band with no end or beginning. As they lie between the rumpled sheets of hot desire, in their master-sized bed, filled with the scent of ecstasy, made for the kings and queens of this precious earth, their naked bodies entwine as one, loving each other like there is no end. Lovemaking so breathless and passionate, it feels like heaven on earth. Their womanhood and manhood firmly connect as the joy of life continues. Then they release their juices from their fountains of undying love, creating an excitement that only they can feel within. Lips in awe as their anxious tongues explore the depth of their mouths, expressing their love in perfect harmony. A language that they have formulated and only they can translate. Their wavy black hair, blazing and clinging to their wet silklike bodies, wrapped in awesome bliss. They reflect the sunshine outside the window, not caring for the formation of day or night. No one cares. This is just us, in our world of paradise. Their legs tightly wrap around each other, like a grapevine that signifies eternal love. They are truly one.

Reflections

As I sit in my lovely, well-appointed bathroom of forgotten royalty, on my famous Lady Di eighteenth-century chair, bequeathed to me by my beloved late great-grandmother, I am reminded of the hero of the Ancient Greeks. In all its glory of golds, which always makes me feel special, high, and mighty, all in one. Adding more drama to my bathroom is my fancy gold magic mirror, which has the power to bring out the beauty of one's inner being, of great splendor, which seems to climb the wall to the ceiling but never touches it. It gives me all the reflections I desire and, fulfilling my fantasies, makes me look wherever and however I want to be. My great-grandmother took great pride in making her granddaughters lovely Christmas and Easter bonnets, with all the fancy trimmings and ribbons of all colors. These memories bring tears of joy, knowing my great-grandmother is no longer with us. God bless her soul.

I am forty years older, and the new reflection in my mirror worries me now. Glossy black hair is replaced with dull-looking gray hair; smooth, soft skin replaced with wrinkles. A youthful face replaced with an aged face. Time waits on no man.

The journey goes on. The question is: how do I accept this change?

Mystery in the Trees

Walking through the forested mountains of Glenmont, admiring the trails of God's creation, I felt at peace. This was on a bright, calm Sunday morning. The breeze was cool, the air was fresh, and the birds were singing sweet melodies. I could also hear the bees buzzing against my enormous, sensitive ears, as well as bats screeching, wild cats mewing, and pigeons cooing. The waterfalls were also nearby, flowing with the most soothing sound. I almost fell asleep walking. How could I ignore the calm sound of flowing water, with small creatures croaking, squeaking, quacking, and enjoying the beauty of the day?

I was most captivated though, with the different characteristics of the trees amid the trees. They somehow appeared overpowering and, to a point, frightening. There were the sweet smells of cedar, pine, spruce, maple, and even some tropical scents that brought back sweet memories of my mountainous homeland. I raised my head and was dazzled by the formation of the rainbow above. The colors of red, bright red, deep red, orange, light and deep, with different shades of green—deep green, peppermint, and so on—hypnotized my state of mind.

"Is it spring or fall?" I verbalized with admiration. Even though I was alone, surrounded by the beauty of nature, I felt comfortable. I wasn't sure, though—I was so mesmerized by the beauty of the forest, something I would not have noticed otherwise. This was a beautiful admiration. I was infatuated. So huge were the trees, I almost lost my thoughts of equanimity (evenness of mind, calmness, composure).

There were so many, but it was all so peaceful, I felt at peace. *A place of solitude*, I thought to myself as I continued walking along the pathways. Pathways so smooth. I felt that I have traveled to an unknown place. I screamed and heard my echo bounce back, not realizing that I was not among other human beings. Breathing freely, I exhaled and inhaled such fresh air traveling through my nostrils, quickly allowing me to gather my thoughts.

Thinking clearly, and making final decisions, I knew they were my friends. No longer afraid, I went forward and touched one of the big barks and said calmingly, "You are my friend," and at that moment, I heard an answer, and I knew I should not fear. This was the sound of the beautiful green branches shaking among each other. Then I knew this was fate. I continued to feel the cool breeze splattering across my face, making me irenic (tending to promote peace). It made my eyes blink, preventing my vision from focusing for a few minutes, but I was too captivated. My silky flowing hair blew in the wind, coming out of form, but I liked the feeling. It was in a style that was unrecognizable. The breeze silently caressed my lips while taking my body on a whirlwind spin, which I welcomed with open arms. Such a relaxing feeling, I was so fascinated. I lost my thought of being. It was at this moment that I wondered, *Can the trees communicate with each other? How old are they? I do not care, but behind the survival of these trees, there is a look of hidden mystery. Observing the daring and strange silence among the trees allows me to sense the mystery that might never be discovered or understood, but I do not care. I have a friend now.*

Loving

True love is formulated within the heart, mind, and soul; it is a renaissance of the soul. True love is felt in every bone within our scared body. True love flows through every vein as it journeys through the body. True love comes from the core of one's heart. True love of the heart, the nesting place, the resting place, where confusion and emotions play games. The mind gets infiltrated. Sense of reasoning is diminished. The eyes of the inner mind, the third eye, stares and watches, not caring for wrong or right, just knowing that the heart is filled with emotions of caring and loving. Wanting to give. Wanting to touch. Wanting to have and needing to have. All senses becoming one—the sense of passion, the sense of wanting, the sense of giving. Engulfed with expression, deep desire. Wanting to be with one's mate. Giving birth to the art of lovemaking.

Desires of a Lonely Woman

Going to bed like a normal human being. Sleeping peacefully during my dreams.

Suddenly waking up from a state of rest into a person no longer me, a ferocious transformation. My body burning like an inferno. Strange desires taking over.

It is as though a creature is invading my body. As the creature takes over, all senses are awakened. Crying out for attention, my nipples get hard and my taunting breast is blown into fullness of trumping desire. Wanting to be touched and sucked.

Anxious fingers brush over my heavily sensual body. A crazy vibration sets in.

Sending my fiery body into hunger, exhilarating hunger, within me. The need to be touched by anyone. A man, woman, animal or anything, to release the rising unbearable hell within me. Opening up the entrance to my womanhood. I started to use my tool of survival, flickering fingers activating and releasing my own hell.

Masturbating my sweet honeycomb until I self-destruct. Yes, yes, my fingers have now become my very best friends. My weapon of choice for survival, slowly and surely releasing my thunderous thrust. I can feel myself reaching my exhilarating peak, my breath staggering, my body vibrating, getting uproarious. That strange sweet feeling of quietude, as if I am about to give birth. Suddenly, short screams burst from my needed lips. My birth water runs down my quivering legs, brings me back, brought me back to earth. Now I know loneliness was the creator of my own hell of upheaval. Never again will I suffer.

I am now man and woman.

Bells of Joy

Bundled up between my thousand-thread-count Egyptian sheets, floating on air, with a softness beyond words, in my masterful king-size bed on this cold winter night.

Dressed in my heavenly birthday suit, breasts fully bloomed, rounded in utmost fullness. Nipples at attention, warm to the touch, ready and willing to be tasted, licked, sucked. Slapped around with a wet tongue from my inner nipple to the outer tip, where the nerve endings are most powerful, injecting uncontrollable raging sensations into my already saturated hairy arena. My body is long and slender, with a waistline to entice any man to do wrong with drunken ecstasy, lying in the dark. A small diamond knob is embedded in my pancake-flat tummy, sparkling in the dark, transforming my body into a precious gem, a single star in the heavens. I run my hands over my lush and very tender pussycat, with harassing fingers teasing my G-spot, jump-starting an array of strange feelings, sending signals that awaken my inner senses of need. It is unbearable, but I am enjoying this congenial moment.

I am pulled out of my dreams into the frightening realization that something is terribly wrong and missing from my life—a man, a soul mate, a warm body to ignite my inner being, taking it to another level. It is the only tool in the universe capable of creating complete satisfaction within one's soul. A rigid iron force, penetrating the center of my being, a man's pride and joy, which makes or breaks him as a man—hunter or human being. Hidden under taunting flesh, laced with honey, sending radar signals to the hidden seed, embedded in my private hairy arena, forcing it to maturity. Pulling it to the surface of life, like a beautiful rose, perfectly made, waiting to be touched and admired while engulfed in the palms of the beholder.

This rose is blooming and spreading with all its glory, with the touch of its Creator.

Living joy expands and brightens to the most marvelous colors of a ripened fruit, ready to be eaten. Yes, this hidden treasure of hell has the power to destroy. Opening the eyes of Eve brings hell on Earth. Brings the devil to his knees, just from a scent and a single touch. Sending caution to the wind, I give my body to this new birth, perfectly formed. Hence, I enter into my fiery hell. Thank heaven for this masterpiece, for the power to create and direct one's joy. It takes me places where only the soul can feel, sending out its scent to infuse body and soul, finally ending with the bells of joy.

The Stranger Next Door

It is a brilliant day, with a ray of sunshine, so startling to the human eye. With no brewing hot air, skies look radiantly blue, evidencing no rain in the forecast anytime soon. The blowing back and forth of the lush green tree branches plays sweet music to my ear. They compete with the sweet chirping sounds of colorful parrots flying loosely in the sky above. A rush of cool breeze, so serene, showers my face with such tenderness. I am sitting in my skimpy summer outfit, making me feel so pampered, just like a spa day. I am enjoying the fullness and the thrill of the moment, rocking and humming away in my own private thoughts. I am sitting in my great-grandma's ancient rocking chair while surveying the cornfields beyond the white picket fence. Suddenly, my chair comes to an abrupt stop. I am having a vision, or perhaps I am in a trance of some sort. Never before have I beheld such a magnificent sight, riding in the cornfield on a beautiful, well-groomed black stallion. He is flashing his enormous black tail with such grace—a magnificent beast indeed! He stands obediently under his master, sitting erectly in his Spanish-style saddle, boldly engraved with the name El Toro. A real stranger to my eyes, a sight to behold, a human being so perfectly made! A stranger dressed in elegantly tailored Spanish riding gear, with cowboy boots, all made especially for a leader. His brimmed hat is fitted on a head that shows a face so stern, with high cheekbones and bushy eyebrows, attractively shaped for a man. Sea-blue razor-sharp eyes that seemed to look through you, with a well-structured, straight, sharp nose, demanding attention. Thick, wide lips, slightly apart, showing brilliant white teeth. So kissable, I think. Wide, erect shoulders, with a broad chest, with every rib showing through his bright white cotton shirt, buttoned halfway, exposing soft, curly black hair traveling along his chest of steel. It raises goose bumps all over my skin, elevating my heart rate, almost drowning out all sound as my ears pound with thrusting desire for this unknown stranger next door.

So stately he sits, with his shirtsleeves rolled tightly around his large, well-built muscles. Such strength he possesses. Closing my eyes, I feel my slender body engulfed with internal rage. My vision blurs with the thought of outstretched arms, holding me tightly but safely riding me into the twilight zone, created just for us, bathing my body and internal soul with a passion locked deeply within us, a secret embedded in our hearts. Parting my lips to receive his darting and anxious tongue deep in my mouth, I suddenly lose consciousness as my mind floats into the outer world from his magical kisses. I am ready to give myself completely. Slowly regaining consciousness, I open my eyes as reality creeps. It was but a dream. A fantasy, a vision in my head—until I glimpse him from the corner of my eye, riding off into the sunset. It is the happiest day of my life—unforgettable memories of the stranger next door, knowing deep in my heart we will meet again!

The Other Side of the Coin

I remember so clearly. I had just turned sweet sixteen, and our friendly neighbors invited me to an older folks' Christmas party. I was so excited to attend to my first real grown-up party that I felt like I was almost grown up myself. I felt all adult-like, with my fancy hairdo. I wore the latest in fashion. Tight white bell-bottom pants, complemented with my favorite white lace off-the-shoulder top, with my sister's borrowed red pumps. I looked great, I thought. Music played loudly, there were lots of buffet-style foods—tasty golden brown chicken, delicious ribs cooked until the meat fell off the bone, served with lots of tasty Screaming Eagle Cabernet Sauvignon wine, delicious Sapphire martini cocktails, and sliced aged vintage cheese. Soon the guests started arriving in their fashionable and sexy red-and-white Christmas colors, with their fancy dancing shoes. Women in stiletto high heels and men in their pointed-toe Versace shoes, all competing among themselves, with their Brackish Pollock men's feather bow ties purchased at the upscale stores.

I will never forget, in the midst of all the excitement, there stood, in the center of the dance floor, the man of my dreams. He was so captivating, so handsome, so striking and well-groomed, that I was spellbound and hypnotized on the spot for a moment. His stunning marble-like brown eyes, that seemed to be pulling me like a magnet, made me fall into a world of trance. He was so well-dressed, in a lovely red embroidered long-sleeve silk shirt. It was most becoming, with white cotton pants and casual white sporty-looking shoes.

Regaining my senses and testing my luck, sending caution to the wind, I walked over and introduced myself. I was not backing down. He accepted my invitation. We began to develop a dialogue. Then the sparks began to fly. We danced all night, which made me the envy of all the ladies in the house. Then the music stopped, and the magic ended. It was time to go home. My prince offered to take me home in his fancy white Maserati sports car, and I agreed, not knowing what danger awaited me. My handsome prince invited me into his brownstone house, nearby a cane field. He reminded me of a gentleman, so I accepted the invitation. I was seated on his soft dark velvet blue sofa. I was offered a cup of Bigelow Cozy chamomile tea. After I took a sip, I remember seeing the change in his demeanor. Then I felt slightly incoherent. He placed a gentle kiss on my lips, which got intense, too intense. He immediately turned into a violent beast. He wanted us to have some quiet time and get to know each other better, against my better judgment. I remember him approaching me like a lion, roaring in hunger, or a prisoner just coming out of bondage for ten years. He approached me vehemently and viciously attacked me. After pushing my seat back into a lying position, I saw danger in his eyes as he tried to rip my pants off, as he viciously tried to rape me. He ripped my underwear from my body, leaving deep flesh scars, as I fought for my life, screaming at the top of my lungs, but to no avail. Savagely, I grabbed and pulled his hair from his scalp, biting into his arm with an empowered force I never knew I possessed, trying to set myself free as he tried to force himself on top of me. Great anger consumed him, as he forced my legs apart like a beast of the jungle, throwing them in midair with the intention of deep penetration with his monstrous weapon of destruction that would truly destroy me forever. I felt motionless. My pounding heart racing out of control, my face glistening with uncontrollable sweat, my nerve endings out of control with deep fear, my eyes flooded with tears.

I whispered a prayer of deliverance, almost breathless, my only hope. At that moment, that very moment, thunderous lightning struck. There were sharp cries of pain from the beast as he rolled over with his hands across his chest. He fell hard on his tiled floor and looked very dead, but I was not going to let that deter my persistent attempts to get to a place of relief.

Heart attack, I thought to myself. My prayers were answered instantaneously. Gathering what was left of my shredded clothing, covering my body with my hands, under the shield of darkness I took off, running against the wind, stopping only for a minute or two to regain my breath. I felt relieved and ran with strength I thought I never had. I fell, but I was able to gain courage to get back on ground, making sure the beast was nowhere in sight and I was safe. Out of shame, this will be my bottled secret for life.

The Magical Quiet Escape Loft

A resting place nestled quietly in the middle of paradise, surrounded by God's glorious beauty of a picturesque island named Jamaica. Flowers of every color and description, flavors sweet-smelling scents that make you feel a sense of love and humility. With the herbs of the earth for every cause consuming you—such peace, tranquility, and memories—I feel so at ease. With every tree, insect, and animal of God's creation at rest, I feel safe. With the wind sailing with such a delicate breeze, I feel a calmness of living. Slowly covering one's face, forcing the fresh air of life into one's nostrils within the stillness of this atmosphere, I am relieved. Inhaling and exhaling, breathing clear thoughts, with a vision for the future, looking at life with a new perspective, I echo.

Stirring the excitement within, we find our needs rising to the surface. Just like Adam and Eve, who lay naked, dangerously and suddenly wanting each other, like a couple who has just experienced holy matrimony. He kisses me with a softness I have never felt before.

I kiss him back with all my heart, with a hardness I never knew I possessed. He raises my taunting breast, with hard nipples ready to be sucked and devoured, as his tongue slowly licks my nipples, from left to right and right to left. He sucks my nipple, inch by inch, until my entire breast is all his, sucking like a hungry babe. I want more. I want him all over me, and just me, alone. Slowly, he moves his free hand slowly, down to my hairy fountain, foamed with lust, massaging my G-spot with such care and tenderness that my body becomes inflamed with reckless need. Forced to grab his hand, I push his patient fingers into my fountain of need, directing it deeper as I scream with vicious pleasure. Never before have I felt such formidable joy, as he continues to bring me happiness, a strange feeling within me, heightened to a powerful explosion, and I scream, "No more."

As I lie panting, he takes my other breast more anxiously. I feel the pleasure of great enthusiasm, elation, and eagerness. In his mouth, sucking away, awaiting my inner feelings once more, there is nothing I can say. It is just passion. This time, he massages my G-spot with his hardness, as he slowly enters my saturated hairy fountain with such domineering ownership, pumping deeper and deeper as I open my shapely legs to receive his great depth. It is such a stabbing joy, such a welcome sharpness that inflames my body. My skin turns fiery red as my whole body blazes with the heat of deep desire. I grab onto him for dear life with legs spread open as far as the eyes can see. I am in heavenly bliss. The magic of this place consumes us as we entwine deeply as one, allowing nothing to pass between us, as we wash our bodies with the sweet perfumed aroma of our sweat. We lose ourselves, speaking in different languages that only we can interpret. Finally, we can take no more, as our bodies explode together, leaving us lifeless, still entwined in each other's arms. Not wanting to withdraw, we can hold back no more. Getting lost in the magic of the magical Quiet Escape Loft is what dreams are made of—dreams that cannot be told, only experienced.

The Mirror of Truth

Looking at my reflection in the Mirror of Truth, I felt a relief of inner peace. It has traveled the world with me, over the oceans and valleys, cities and towns, near and far, triggering memories of the past.

How can I forget? In my twenties strolling along the streets of Trench Town, Kingston, a small town in Jamaica, with my butt round and pompous, giving a polemic view. Hot and sexy was I in my tight stretch jeans, just the way the men like to see it, young and old, from their bicycles, motorbikes, and cars. Or just standing there watching me walk by with my small round breasts, standing firm in my low-cut bra, exposing my printed nipples in full view, through my thin strapless summer blouse, tightly fitted to my shapely body. Walking tall, with perfectly sculptured and shapely legs in my red heels, my slender model figure filled with confidence, feared by married women, who were there to hold onto their partners for life—a husband, a man, their baby-father—without success. It was impossible with a body like mine. There would be no match. Thinking of all the naughty acts they would like to do, or try to do, to me, I secretly internalized. Taking my clothes off before any man would set off fireworks without the Fourth of July. Their bodies would be on fire, creating their own fireworks of excitement and joy, fighting erections that exploded with impatience. Looking at their faces with their idiotic expressions from ecstasy, I pitied them. I am queen in my own right. I crack the whip, on my terms. I was ripe for the picking with youth, marked all over my cute, dainty face, with kissable red lips, straight nose, big bright eyes, and fiery red hair, rolled up in a bob, the latest hairdo.

Now, at age seventy, the Mirror of Truth shows something different. My once cute, youthful face is now filled with wrinkles, eyes marked with strong lines and fading eyesight. My once-lovely full head of hair now looks like a ball of snow. My slender body now looks somewhat like a skeleton, but my inner desire continues to flow, leaving me needy, wanting to be touched and held tightly, to feel that powerful weapon moving back and forth, anxiously, inside me, an experience with no recovery, leaving me standing alone to seek my own comfort to satisfy my needs. This time, no admirers, no onlookers, no men stopping with intent, forcing me to market myself or find myself on the shelf. What a difference age makes!

Believing in Your Dreams

Clara Young was considered a nutcase, always daydreaming of love on earth, in the clouds. Her prince arriving one day, but she was my very dear friend for many years. Short and stubby but shapely, with a bouncy butt, shaped like two watermelons joined together side by side, she never failed to attract the sound of a whistle. She was beautiful, with reddish-orange hair that stood out and made a statement. Most of her life, she lived a lonely life, devoting herself to the care and upkeep of her grandmother Lacy, who was old and frail. She took her to Sunday services, which were a must so she could socialize with her dear and only friends.

She also kept her little cottage, built in the eighties, spotless and homey, on a half an acre of land in the picturesque countryside of Rockaway Bay. Greenery as far as the eyes could see, trees of all heights and shapes, with their colorful leaves swaying in the high winds but holding on and seeming never to fall. Birds of colors flew from limb to branch, while deer jumped over fallen branches and fences, with young ones in tow. Small creatures ran scared, up and under the trees.

However, the flower garden was her pride and joy. She planted, nourished, and cherished those plants, giving them all her love. They were her family, but they were now overgrown due to a short illness. Clara Young needed help. An advertisement for a gardener was placed in the daily news to help Clara maintain her gracious garden. Sitting patiently in her newly built swing on her front porch, she waited for her first caller to arrive. Something startling caught her interest as she stared at the passersby. Walking down her overgrown driveway, before a ray of sunlight, was a tall figure of a man. He had golden corn-like hair that shone brightly in the sunlight, which also shone directly on her flowered blouse. He had a brilliant smile, showing lovely white teeth.

He caught her eye as he stood there in his white muscle T-shirt, showing heavyweight muscles, looking so powerful in his blue jean shorts, exposing his legs, like those of a well-bred stallion. He was wearing rugged working boots, walking with strong strides and lunch pack hanging over his right shoulder. She swallowed long and hard. This was her long-awaited prince. Combing nervous fingers through her curly red hair, she walked slowly to the gate to greet him, looking up into his sea-blue eyes. She was spellbound for a moment. *This cannot be happening*, she thought. On her birthday, May 26, a true gift from God.

Asking questions was a waste of time, as no sound came, but he understood. He, on the other hand, appeared nervous as well, despite his relaxed outlook. They hastened to sign language for a short while, both sweating but appearing to understand each other.

Dreams are real.

The stranger standing before her was the same as the man in her dreams. Strangely, they both felt an odd connection, leaving both with questions in their eyes.

This is what dreams are meant for!

Being a Cougar

Ha, life.

I'm sitting in my favorite Bassett antique wing chair, on my gigantic bedroom hardwood floor. Staring out my window into the bright sunshine, I wonder, am I making the right decision dating James and bearing the name "cougar"?

The new man in my life is from Jamaica, a sunny island in the Caribbean surrounded by clear blue sea, which they call the Land of Sunshine. Never before have I met a human being so pure and filled with affection. His adoration for flowers, pets, and children took my breath away. His little son, Roger, approximately seven years old, who lost his mother to cancer, clings to his father so affectionately. They go everywhere with his well-trained puppy, La La, who is always playfully wagging his tail. They live in a small basement apartment, scarcely furnished, with the minimal everyday needs, but it is comfortable, with love felt throughout. He is a hardworking man, with his handiwork, made with his own hands, on display.

These are the qualities that captured my heart. Yet he is fifteen years my junior, so full of life, with great sexual needs. Will I be able to cope? What will happen when I am in my sixties and he is in his forties? Will he still be attracted to me, as he is now? Will I be able to meet his demands in bed, making him happy? Now, at age forty, I am struggling to keep up with his fitness. He is so active, playing football on weekends, almost all day, entertaining his buddies, having late-night parties. Sometimes I wonder how his life can endure such pressure—still going to work early in the morning, still wanting and able to cope with the sex before he leaves. He calls it an "appetizer" and "energy medicine." I must say, he is good, a real-life fine cracker. There are times when I refuse him and feel qualms all day about it, questioning myself.

Was I wrong to refuse him? Will I lose him?

I love him so much. He is not only good-looking, with straight black hair, but he has all the various qualities I desire. Perfect playful fingers, so soft to the touch. Straight, stubborn-looking nose that portrays a strong personality. Muscles of steel that hug me so tightly in bed. Dark, smooth-looking chocolate skin that hypnotizes my heart. He never fails to give me goose bumps all over. His strong, well-groomed body brings me such comfort. I curl up into his powerful arms like a babe.

My friends say he is too young for me. It will not last, and he might be after my money, which I do not have. My deep gut feeling says otherwise. Based on this, I have decided to trust my instincts. It is my life, my happiness, my decision. It is the biggest gamble of my life, a leap of faith that I have chosen to take, throwing caution to the wind.

He brings me happiness, takes away my fears, keeps me safe, and shows me respect. This is all I need. I have decided to face the challenges of the future. This is my happiness.

So "cougar" it will be.

The Risk of Cheating

Is it worth the risk? Why do men cheat? Are they sex-starved human beings on a mission or just plain hunters trying to score so they can be popular among their friends?

So it was with Calvin Chase, a young thirty-five-year-old native from a small town in Africa. Calvin was born in a culture where men rule and women are their eternal slaves. Tall, dark, and handsome, he thought he was God's blessing to all lonely women. He was a cheater who learned the consequences the hard way.

Calvin was self-employed, a dedicated homebuilder, married, with twins—Alec and Annie—who looked just like their him, sporting curly dark hair and sharp-looking eyes that drew one's attention. His wife was a lovely, hardworking woman who was almost as tall as he was, at six feet tall, with golden blonde hair. She had the most amazing statuesque figure, which was the main attraction to him. He adored and trusted her wholeheartedly. She took exceptional care of their children. They were well-groomed and well-mannered, and any parent would have been proud of them.

When he cheated, returning home late most nights, he would feel guilty, knowing he had been neglecting his wife for some time. But then he thought she would always be home, because that is how he thought of her—naïve. There was no need to worry about their relationship. This he felt confident of. They considered themselves true and committed Christians, regularly attending church at the only Baptist church building, just a block away from home. In a small community on a hill, called Marymount, home to a small group of hardworking civilians, he participated in church activities and was well-known in his community as a good and respectable tradesman and family man. Unknown to anyone, Calvin had a well-guarded secret. He enjoyed extracurricular activities outside marital life with other women. This surprised the little community of Marymount. Whether married, single, or dating, they all presented an exciting risk that he was willing to take, but he did not always come out on top.

His latest victim was a vibrant, self-absorbed twenty-seven-year-old girl named Shelly McCoy. She thought she was the cat's pajamas, always walking by his job site, next door to her neighbor's house, in much-too-tight clothing, but damn, she looked good. She gave signs of being available, attracting a challenge for Calvin, who was eager to score. He lived just a mile away, but this did not deter him. The challenge was his, and conquer her he would after a few weeks of small talk and a couple of dinner dates. Eventually, they became close. She was unemployed and was sharing an apartment with her husband, a policeman, until she could find a job. After a while, he learned of her employment status. Strangely, he was never introduced to her husband or invited over when he was home. they lived on the fourth floor of a neatly built redbrick apartment building. She had lived there for the past six months. This suited Calvin, considering he was a married man and had no desire to look into the eyes of justice. Finally, on a Friday afternoon, filled with roaring thunder and hailing rainfall, his job site was forced to be closed early. He was invited over by Shelly for a shot of Suntory

Hibiki twenty-one-year-old whiskey, a very expensive liquor, or so she claimed.

However, upon his arrival, she greeted him dressed only in a hot red leatherette, a vogue raincoat, which revealed her stark-naked sculptured body, with red-bottom high-heel Christian Louboutin shoes. This was instant dynamite. He had an immediate calling from his manhood, resulting in an embarrassing huge burgeon bulge from his khaki pants that could not be overlooked. Her well-rounded, taunting breasts, with teasing nipples protruding from a perfectly sculptured body, did little to keep his sweet rebellion under control. Walking into the apartment in an almost hypnotic state, entranced by her supreme beauty, he dropped his overloaded workbag in a haphazard manner and leaped into her arms, kissing her anxious parted lips viciously. He danced her toward the newly painted white walls, where he pinned her motionless inflamed body, deep, deep moans of passion escaping manipulating lips, formulating a language only they could translate. Sweet sweat poured unremittingly down their bodies, and soon they were unable to withstand the inferno. Her coat fell unscrupulously to her feet, exposing a soft, delicate, body unparalleled to any other he had seen. His khaki shirt almost ripped during its hasty removal, thrown up into the heated atmosphere, landing on a place of its choosing. There was no time or need for a bed, as their needs were immediate. Bouncing against naturally heated white walls, he profusely and valiantly entered his very saturated domain, filling the room with uproarious screams as they reached their formidable peak, which left them clinging with deadly intensity to each other. Finally debilitated, they stood lifeless in each other's arms.

A smile formed on his lips, as he knew his mission was accomplished. He reluctantly pulled away, knowing time was against him to return home. Stepping into the bathroom for a quick wash, he returned to find Shelly lying naked on the sofa, almost dozing off. He kissed her lightly on her forehead. Preparing to take his exit, he became distracted with the sound of keys rattling in the door lock. Seeing the sudden change of color on her fearful face, he knew he had stepped into the danger zone. Quickly his bag was pushed behind the sofa, against the wall, where she lay. Then she urgently grabbed him, out of desperation, with shaky hands, and pushed him under the very low bed of their one-bedroom apartment. This was the only safe haven, but it made movement almost impossible. Left in a perturbed state, he wondered if she was having an affair or if she was trying to set him up.

His worst fear was answered shortly, when the stranger addressed Maria as "my lovely wife."

"How was your day?" she asked sheepishly.

"Why are you naked?"

"I was about to take a shower" was her too-quick reply.

"You never fail to arouse me, dressed or naked," a smooth voice claimed.

Next, there was a long silence, followed by a big bang on the bed. This was followed by intimate moans and rumbling on the bed, inches above his head. His only escape from injury was to stick his face into the dusty floor. Never before had he been so close to captivity. Faces of his young twins and lovely wife flashed before his eyes. How was he going to get out alive? Sleeping with a policeman's wife, a man who carries a gun, was not a good idea. Shaking nervously now, in wet underwear, he prayed silently, making a pact with God to save him, promising in return that this would be his last unfaithful mission. To his relief, the traumatic rumbling above stopped, and the stranger headed for the bathroom. A few minutes later, which seemed like hours, Calvin was signaled that it was safe to leave. This was the most inconceivable thing any woman had ever done to him. This was indeed a call too close for comfort. Closed eyes were now opened to the light and the lurking dangers of cheating.

Calvin went home a new man, with a different point of view on cheating, his appetite for new flesh and challengers faded.

Secrets within the Walls

Growing up in Largo, Maryland, as a small child in a Christian community, we were brought up to worship God as King of all people. The pastor, as God's helper, was given the utmost respect. Everyone knew each other and believed in what our pastor taught us. No sex before marriage. No kneeling to temptation. No foreplay. Listen to your parents and follow the teachings of your pastor. I knew no other life on Sundays. We all went to church, worshiping together, visiting the sick and shut-ins, praying with them, and bringing small donated baskets of food.

My father, as pastor, conducted two services on Sundays. He counseled those with marital and other personal issues after church. Members would drop by unannounced, giving us good wishes and gifts, showing appreciation for the sermon that day. It was an event I always prayed would end soon so dinner could be served. Being out all day, I was starved. My father would be gone for days and weeks at a time—on church seminars abroad and visiting other churches when at home. My mom and I were left to conduct services until he returned.

At age twenty-one, I got engaged to the assistant pastor. He was handsome, very becoming, smart, totally committed to the church and the ways of the Bible. This relationship was approved by our parents and the devoted congregation. Soon after that, we were married and conceived a little boy name Ken. A year later, my father died, and the assistant pastor, my husband, was promoted to pastor. This changed our lives. As pastor, his responsibilities increased. We no longer ate as a family. He traveled regularly. When he was home, our phone rang before daylight and after dust. There were the sick to visit, at home and in the hospital, and sermons to write. I did my best to support him, but it was a tiresome job. While caring for a young child, no one seems to think a pastor gets tired or has his own life to live.

This left me standing alone. Too many weeks and months without love and affection. I became needy, starving for love and affection. I started to stray in my thoughts. This was wrong, but I was out of control. I prayed for forgiveness, forced to create my own world of affection. There were nights when my husband was out of town, I would lie in bed naked, looking at my reflection in our huge wall mirror, massaging my breasts, arousing the hardness of my nipples, whispering deeply under my breath for someone to come through my bedroom door. I did not care if it is the plumber or the gardener, as long as they had a big, hard manhood to stick in my suffering, anxious vagina, to release my burning pressure of need. I would open my legs wide and stare into the mirror, sticking my fingers in deep, back and forth, pretending my imaginary friend was on top of me, copulating me without mercy.

Yes, I was starved for sex. I was not ashamed. Our sex life was nonexistent. My need was never noticed. From the moment we said our vows, I knew I had made the biggest mistake ever. He was truly dedicated to the church, being a pastor's son. I, on the other hand, just wanted a respectable husband and to be respected. Our sex life was never the greatest. He was old school. He wanted to do nothing new or creative in our lovemaking apart from what the

Bible instructed. He said I should never show neediness or lust. He would come to me when the time was right. My heart sank at those words, but the damage was already done. I went into my private corner and prayed for God to see me through. Going to church with a big, happy-looking smile, at my husband's side, pretending we had a perfect life, was becoming unbearable. Having my own private sessions with my imaginary friend was my way of coping as a pastor's wife with my spells of loneliness.

He is a good man, I still love him, and I will continue to stand by him, with my secret held tightly hidden within these sacred walls.

Saying Goodbye

There is always bitterness in a relationship, but on the flipside, there is also love, forgiveness, and appreciation.

When Ken, a single man in his mid-fifties, met Lorraine at his friend Joe's annual summer pool party, he felt as if he had just won a million dollars. She was captivating as she lay by the pool. She looked so radiant under the glowing sunshine. Her shoulder-length hair glistened, and she had a most becoming natural smile that took his breath away. As she lay there, wearing only her yellow bikini swimwear bottoms, she was a sight to behold. Her exposed well-rounded breasts were intoxicating, leaving him speechless and sending hot flashes through his body. It took great strength to pull himself together. Her big, luscious breasts were perfectly formed, with a golden tan complexion. She had long, slender, sculptured legs. Her toenails were polished hot red, ready to be taken. What a feast that would be. Slowly, he began to approach her, wondering if he would be ignored or fought off by a hidden admirer. He took the gamble and won.

Standing over this glowing goddess, he offered to apply her suntan lotion. To his great surprise, she accepted with unbelievable ease. He immediately took the opportunity to introduce himself and struck up a conversation. To his astonishment, he discovered they had a lot in common. Due to their common interest, they speedily developed a loving relationship, having regular date nights. They would sit under the stars in Lorraine's magical home garden, where they both enjoyed the solitude and the mystery of the moment. Their brewing love and deep feelings for each other brought them to a decision to move in together.

They would soon learn each other's faults and shortcomings. Six months into the relationship, jealousy started to kick in due to Ken's possessiveness. He was an older man. She was a younger woman with lots of admirers. His insecurities were the beginning of a very uncomfortable home atmosphere. As a result, neither wanted to be home. On a very wet Sunday morning, with a strange stillness in the air, they were listening to the heavy downpour of the rainfall. The winds were flying high. They vividly viewed the deserted streets through their frosted kitchen windows while having their usual morning coffee. The phone rang on the kitchen wall. It was for Lorraine. Ken eavesdropped, hearing a man's voice in the background. This angered Ken, and he accused Lorraine of being unfaithful. She tried as hard as she could to convince him otherwise but to no avail.

At the end of their bitter and harassing conversation, Ken angrily threw down his teacup with a heavy bang on the tea table, sending it shattering on the white tiled floor. He gingerly walked through the door in a dangerous rage, leaving Lorraine in bewilderment. That night, he did not return home for dinner, which was out of character, but Lorraine sighed and went ahead having dinner alone, thinking he was just still upset with her. But deep down in her gut, she felt uncomfortable, and for some strange reason, she knew something was wrong. No matter what happened between them, he never missed dinner. Shortly afterward, the phone rang. She jumped up with shaky feet, feeling numb. For the first time in their relationship, she felt a sense of fear.

Finally mustering the courage to answer the phone, with nervous hands and hoarseness in her voice, she said, "Hello."

It was the police on the other end of line, telling her that her husband had died of an heart attack. She needed to identify the body. Standing dumbfounded, looking at the phone in her hands, she burst out crying uncontrollably. She screamed at the top of her lungs, which could be heard a mile away. While she cried with painful tears flooding her face and blinding her eyes, she began to pray that he would be received through the heavenly gates, forcing the caller to hang up due to the deafening noise.

She could not believe he was gone—no goodbyes, hugs, kisses, or even a final "I love you." She closed her eyes for a cherished moment for a glance at the past. After months of sleepless nights and sad memories at not being able to say goodbye, she finally came to the heart-wrenching conclusion that maybe it was for the best. This rested heavily on her mind, an everlasting, unrelenting memory that would be with her for life.

Heartbreak

I remember the moment I saw him, so tall and good-looking, with thick, well-shaped black eyebrows stretched to the corners of his eyes. How cute they made him look, giving me the urge to touch them. His boyish fade haircut gave him that prominent military look, and his rich, creamy chocolate-colored skin, with sparkling white teeth, made his face glow when he smiled. I knew he was mine. With a fluttering heart and severe anxiety taking over, I wondered how I would make my move. Finally, with order pad in hand and adjusting my nametag on my uniform, I plunged forward, politely introducing myself and offering to take his order.

At first, he ignored my presence, as he dialed his phone. Finally, I got his full attention. There was an undenied spark of interest from the flow of his eyes, running over me as he disconnected his phone and rested his eyes on my nametag.

"Ms. Piper's Cheesecake Factory Employee of the Year," he said.

"That's correct," I replied.

The rest was history. We began a whirlwind love affair. He was a prominent businessman, so money was not an object. I was treated like a princess, in need of nothing. Valentine's Day, I was showered with the largest bouquet of red and pink roses I had ever seen, delivered to my job. I felt proud and special that all my coworkers could see that I was very special to someone. There were questioning, envious eyes. We dated for a year. At one point, marriage was mentioned, leaving me hopeful that the relationship would finally one day head to the altar. I was happy and so very sure of myself and the relationship. Then, when the big New Year's Eve party preparation came around, I naturally did likewise. I jumped up in preparation for the big party, spending above my normal limits, wanting to be his Cinderella.

Suddenly, there was a big change in our relationship. He became difficult to reach at work. Did not return phone calls and stopped visiting me. I was frantic, reaching out to his family and friends, fearing something had happened to him. But I was only told he was busy.

On New Year's Eve, the biggest event of the year, I was left deserted, standing in the middle of my disarrayed bedroom with my beautiful gown looking down at me from my closet door, where it stood in all its glory. In bewilderment and confusion, I could only listen to the crowds through my bedroom window, bringing the New Year in with songs and screams of merriment. Drunk and carefree people were having the time of their life. Never before had I been so heartbroken. Never before had I felt such intense emptiness throughout my body. My heart felt as if it had been lifted out of place and ripped to pieces. So deeply inflicted was my pain. I could not feel my intensities, but I knew severe damage had been done. Where had I gone wrong? What had I done? Was I at fault? No answers came forth.

Two days later, I received a visit from my Prince of Darkness, who emptied my life and threw my heart out of alignment, changing me into a being I did not recognize, bringing me the news that had gone back to his first love, who had returned from overseas and back into his life. And he told me how very sorry he was. I detected no remorse or sadness in his once-adorable brown eyes. At this moment, I was hit by the realization that I was living in a make-believe world, a world I wanted to believe in. I was too in love to see the signs. I was nothing but a pastime, a bit of entertainment for him until his true love returned. How could I have been so blind? Why me? With my broken heart and tears rising in my eyes, which I refuse to let fall, I walked away in a daze, knowing it was nothing but a dream.

All in my delusional head.

The Code of Understanding

Loneliness, the culprit of devastating life decisions. Do you know what's it like to be truly alone? No family. No real friends. No one who cares. Just work to home, every week, every month. Sleeping alone, wrapped up under the sheets, lifeless sheets. Masturbating oneself. Not being able to feel the real hardness of a man's luscious organ. Penetrating you deeply. Taking you to the land of ecstasy. Not having the softness of your breasts ruffled with hard, firm hands. Delicate tongue licking your nipples. Anxious thick lips sucking the fullness of your breasts, like a babe on its mother's breast. The needs that lead one astray. The comfort of a married man insisting on satisfaction, knowing there is someone caring. But knowing where you stand. One giving pleasure. One receiving momentum happiness, with desires of longing and hunger fulfilled. No heartbreak. No pain. No disappointment. No serious love commitment. Just an understanding. An agreement in silence between two lonely people, searching for love and fulfillment.

A code of understanding that brings a peaceful ending.

Listen to Your Heart

Sunbathing in my luscious, flawless work of art, my formidable birthday suit, created and formulated by the mystery of the heavens. A delicate sponge-like skin, as that of a new babe. Such purity. The intimate dream of any man to touch and devour under this magnificent, heavenly sunset, richly formed of an array of brilliant colors, seeping under the clouds as far as the eyes will flow. What a picturesque sight indeed. So daring was this magical moment, as I lay carefree on this warm white innocent patch of sand, being soaked up by this masterpiece of God's heavenly work. Thoughts and visions of my uncertain life swimming in my confused and exhausted mind. A future filled with uncertainties, to step forward into the unpredicted future. I was born to be free, like the blue waters of the ocean sails in on monstrous waves. Ready to wash away the piece of the shores with birds of wonder, flying freely and undisturbed above. Should I stay and live with my doubts? Or should I listen to my heart and move onto higher grounds, experiencing what true life is all about and taking my chances, setting my soul as free as the ocean? Indeed I will. Listening to my heart is the stepping stone, into the future and the unknown.

The Vow

We promise to love, honor, obey, and cherish on that special day.

At that emotional and tender cherished moment. 'Til death do us part. But somewhere along the line, souls get lost and memories forgotten. It is too long a time to hold on to each other. As life's hardship take their toll on us. One happy, loving memory, so hard to remember and hold onto. Where are our true values placed in life? As we age, so does our marriage. I wonder. I wonder, was it the excitement in the air? Or were we ever truly in love at that special moment? How is true love measured? By the minute, hour, day, or year? Does anyone really know?

True Identity

How well do you know your husband? How much do you trust your husband?

How well do you know your neighbor? Is he loyal? Is he faithful? Shelly Ann, happily married for ten years to a husband she loved, a man she trusted and thought she thoroughly knew, was in for the shock of her life.

On a bright, sunny Monday morning, after rising from a blissful and most satisfying night with her husband, she began her chores of getting his lunch ready for work. She then kissed him goodbye before starting her daily household chores. At noon, she decided to visit her very good friend, and friendly neighbor, a sexy redheaded female she had known for three years. She brought with her a piece of oven-hot apple pie she had made. After ascending the steps, she pushed her neighbor's door open, as she usually does, knowing she lived alone and had no lovers she knew of. There was no sign of her friend in the kitchen. She headed for the bedroom, and without notice, or knocking, she pushed the door open. She was completely surprised at what she came across. Quickly, as quickly as she opened it, she closed the door, surprised, with a smile on her face, that her friend had never shared her secret.

Later that afternoon, when her husband arrived from work, Shelly Ann told him of her experience with her neighbor and friend—how dumbfounded and surprised she was as she glimpsed her neighbor in bed with a strange man. Adding to her confusion, her husband only asked, in a very serious tone, one she had never heard before, if she knew her neighbor's lover.

To his quietly listening ear and personal inner joy and triumphant victory, she replied, "No, but he strongly reminded me of you, but I knew you were at work."

Close call, he thought with a giant grin on his face of betrayal.

Can you ever be sure of the man who sleeps next to you? she thought.

Survival Techniques

Is it possible to be happily married with kids and still be lonely, with a void in your life? So it was with Carla Price, a lovely Mexican native, with flowing black hair that blew so gracefully with the wind. She had an exquisite face, created with a permanent smile and a physique to die for. She was a stay-at-home mom, well supported by her military husband, stationed abroad for the past two years in Peru. He saw to it that his lovely wife had every comfort to suit her needs. What else would any woman want? Carla met her husband, Chris, while working for a large supermarket chain. After a year of whirlwind romance, he proposed. He then asked her to resign her job to become a full-time housewife, as she was now expecting. This was a dream come true after working all her life, coming from a poor and very needy family.

Their marriage was bliss. Having their first child, named Jack, bought utter joy to them both. Their sex life was more than she expected. He was a small-built man but rigid in frame, who took his job quite seriously and was well respected! The first time they made love was a shocker to her. He was physically fit in every muscle, showing power of strength and fitness, but what he displayed between his legs, built like that of a stallion, got her a little nervy. In her head, she wondered frantically, was she capable of receiving such a generous package? He proceeded to seduce her with his tender, intense kisses, from her ears to her lips. From her nipples to the passionate spunky sucking of her breast. Running playful fingers along her G-spot between her legs. Sending shocking rage throughout her body, forcing out involuntary screams of pleasure as she grabbed onto his strong arms for dear life. Pushing his fingers deeper into her valley of ecstasy. She began moaning and begging him to fully inject her now. The droughts she previously had were no longer as he slowly entered and devoured her passage. He held so tightly, with such proclivity and proprietorship, as he claimed his price. She screamed with readiness, acceptance, and pure pleasure as he rode her home. It ended in a frightening explosive landing for both. Wet and exhausted, they thanked each other in silence before falling asleep entwined.

These are the memories and pleasures Clara had craved during her two years of waiting. Having a husband who provides well is one thing. Having a husband at home on a regular basis is a big difference. She learned that the hard way. Night after night, she lay in bed with torching emptiness only she could describe. No gentle touch giving her that pleasant sensation and desire. No playful fingers combing through her hair, relaxing her. No sensational tongue massages lingering along her neck. No tender licking of her nipples flooding desires within. No anxious sucking of her breasts, drawing pulsating vibrations within her vagina. She missed all these personal life comforts and needed them desperately. This forced her into survival of her demon-like desires. Her insight, imagination, and creativity kicked in, saving her from self-destruction and divorce. She discovered the magic and power of forceful running water, how relaxing it could be opening up her pores, which provided a rejuvenating feeling, pumping up her lurking inner desires to the surface, igniting deep sexual needs. The power and magic of a forceful flow from the shower head.

It sent a corrupting, vicious sensation up into the walls of her craving and starving vagina, heavenly laid with need, ending with a most satisfying suction eruption.

This experience is no substitution for the lovemaking her husband serviced her with, but it helped with the cravings and prevented her from being an unfaithful wife. Yes, indeed, her own personal survival technique.

Definition of Love

Love is deep, embedded everlasting unguarded passion that rips through the inner you. Love is untouchable as the breath we re-breathe. Love is no respect of woman, man, or child. Love is as unapproachable as our thoughts. Love is a circle, never-ending. Love is as demanding as the demon within us. Love creates joy and removes pain. Love cannot be held like the cool breeze that blows around us. Love cannot be contained like the waves of the ocean. Love floats among us and within us. Love is a special heavenly key that unlocks the lonely heart and painful hearts.

Love knows no fear or hate. Love is the main valve of the heart, bringing joy, happiness, and hope, a feeling of rejuvenation uplifting the spirit to great heights. Without love, our lives would be empty. Thriving on hope is love. Getting a second chance is love. Feeling free is love. Love is living our values every day.

The Gullible Woman

How can we expect a woman born in poverty, living in poverty all her life, not be gullible? She was welcome unto this earth. Born as a babe in a wooden hut, under limited candlelight. Barely enough towels and sanitation amenities. Growing up only knowing to live off the little her mother could offer, as no father could be found. Odds jobs are rare, and wages are barely enough to feed her little ones. Stealing became a habit and pattern of survival. Going on odd jobs washing and ironing large bags of clothes. Sometimes not even being offered a meal after a laborious workday, as well as not earning enough to take home. After transportation, being forced to walk home or find other means. So she turned to her second option, the oldest known to man. Turning to man, a stranger, who made false promises, who appeared nice to her and sounded good, because she needed extra support for her little ones.

The money will come for a short while, as well as another fatherless babe. A gullible woman only knows what she was born into. Not educated enough to figure out her mistakes. Just knowing she needs to find a way to feed her family and have a roof over her head. All these children in tow, only encouraging more poverty.

Born in poverty and die in poverty, unless we open our hearts, reach out, and give. These poor souls richly deserve a second chance at life.

Denial

We were all delivered on this planet as healthy babes, through the blessed wombs of our God-given mothers. Nursed and nourished with natural nutrients. Embedded in the fountain of our mother's nipples. Cared for from the sweat of our mothers and fathers, who provide our daily meals and a roof over our heads. Brought through rugged times with God's guidance to become children of proud parents. Setting the stage for future mothers and fathers ourselves. Then the aging process starts all over again. Our men refusing to accept change. Refusing to step out of the shoes of the young. Continuing to pursue young women. Fooling themselves that time can stand still, bringing forth their second-generation set of kids. Deserting their wives and marriages for younger women, only to have it thrown in their faces with embarrassment after spending their life savings to impress and buy out the younger women to no avail. Unable to face and embrace the fact that they can no longer walk in the shadow of the young, being unable to fulfill the sexual and daily demands, as the young would, due to degenerative health from the aging process.

Thinking young, pretending to be young, and feeling needed by the young, allowing them to go against the process of aging. In their mind's eye.

Daily Blessings

Waking up above ground being able to welcome the bright, glorious sunshine, with open arms for family and friends, unlike the many unfortunate souls sleeping peacefully beneath the sacred earth. Thank you, Lord. We wake up, having survived the devastating storm that passed while we slept. Thank you, Lord. We wake up able to see your reflection in the mirror after threatening eye surgery. Thank you, Lord. We wake up with our whole family, safe and sound around our bed after surviving a near-death car crash. Thank you, Lord. We wake up to hear the doctor say, "All your tests are normal. You can go home today," after a long stay in the hospital. Thank you, Lord. We wake up to find our sick child no longer in danger's arms. Thank you, Lord.

Your difficult pregnancy has ended, and your babe is safe and beautiful, screaming loudly. Thank you, Lord. Despite all the crimes and fears of this cruel world, waking up to be a great-grandfather or great-grandmother. Thank you, Lord. I wake up to hear the amazing chattering of the birds, unlike so many people of my delicate age, unable to enjoy this entertainment of nature. Thank you, Lord. Blessings held dear to our hearts. We will never be able to repay or say, "Thank you" enough.

Amen.

A Man's World of Lust and Deceit

In days gone by, when there was lots of love and respect to our individual partners, being honest and sincere. Having date nights heading to courtship, marriage, then intimacy and a family unit. Family interacting with their children's private lives, giving constant guidance, which they appreciated. Keeping them on a straight path.

What went wrong? The hands of time have changed. Families separating their children. Lives in turmoil with high divorce rates and unfaithful husbands on the rise. So it was with Susan, a hard-working single migrant from Jamaica. Working two jobs, one as a private duty nurse, taking care of the elderly in their private homes on the weekends, which gave her a chance to rest. This was unlike her day job as a dialysis technician in a clinic, monitoring patients with kidney failure on the dialysis machine, a tedious job. Working restlessly to take care of her family, which she left behind on the small Caribbean island nation of Jamaica. Employment and poverty are at a very high rate. No proper running water, escalated food prices from constant droughts, poor housing, and a high crime rate.

Susan wanted a better life for herself and family, so she migrated to the United States of America, the land of opportunity, to fulfill her dreams. She has always worked with little or no rest. This lifestyle was beginning to show on her. Her face was looking drawn, her hair untidy, her clothes shabby, not having the time for proper attire. This concerned her best friend, Nadia, who thought it was time for her to have a man in her life to share some of the burden and create some fun for her. So she had her boyfriend, Steve, a pharmacist and a married man, but separated. So she was told. He took excellent care of her. So why should she worry about his private life? The sex was satisfying, and her rent was being paid on time every month. She was living a life she could not afford on her own, in a skyscraper apartment on the twentieth floor in a very highly rated neighborhood, with all the amenities of good living. The price for sharing a bed with a married man, receiving this treatment. Who cared if he was married or not? A blind date was set up with his best friend, James, who was a lover in every right. Tall, dark, and handsome, with no loss for words. He greeted Susan at her door with a bottle of Caymus Cabernet Special Selection red wine and red roses and planted a quick, surprising kiss on her lips as soon as she opened the door. Stunned, she stood motionless for a second before stepping back and letting him in. A quick introduction was made before leaving for their date. He took her dancing at a popular night spot to the sound of calypso music, and it was like a breath of fresh air. For once, she felt free and happy. An unforgettable memory. She arrived home late morning. He kissed her goodbye, and all the magic of the night was over. Waking up with the memories of the night brought eagerness to see him again. Strangely, she had time at bedtime, falling asleep on the phone at times.

Soon a second date was arranged. This time it would be dinner at his apartment. Spotless and well-furnished. Too neat, and a little feminine, she thought. To her surprise, he prepared his own meal, comprised of baked chicken, sweet potatoes, and mixed vegetables, with a small apple pie for dessert. The expected red bottle of wine was attractively placed on a romantically arranged table. Scented candles were lit with sparking lights flowing as she looked at him across the table. Through the candlelight, she sensed the most romantic feeling. She felt excitingly special at that moment. After dinner, they danced to soft romantic music, setting the pace for the night as she danced with her head resting on his broad shoulders. She felt safe, with no care in the world. As the night passed on, they kept getting closer and closer to the bedroom, a sign of intent. Finally, half-drunk and half-conscious, she was lying in his bed with panties being delicately removed, with him kneeling over her, trapped by his powerful legs. With his amazingly huge weapon of pleasure, despite his slender structure, fully erect, creating an excitement that engulfed her sensual body like live electrical current. She wanted him. She looked into his eyes. He had a curt smile on his lips. He understood. Kneeling forward, he kissed her anxiously, his tongue blocking any sound as his hand slowly explored her body unexpectedly. Cautiously, he released his tongue, exploring her neck, upward to her ear. He went downward to her breasts hastily, licking her nipples before engulfing her breasts with one deep breath, with such urgency. A quiet scream escaped her breathlessly as his eager fingers lingered in her bushy arena. He landed on that special spot, igniting a madness she had never felt before. Recklessly, she called him with her needy body as she spread her legs nervously, but anxiously, apart to consecrate this glorious, long-awaited moment.

So, powerfully and triumphantly, he drove into her successfully, bringing her to a place she had never been before, and back, exploding like fireworks. Finally, they gracefully landed, falling asleep, entwined and exhausted, lying in each other's arms, saying their final goodbyes in the dawn of the morning. Suddenly an anxious knock from the front door could be heard. She glanced questionably at him, thinking it might be her neighbor in need of help. Looking somewhat angry, he hurriedly grabbed his robe and ran downstairs—just as someone kicked in the door. There was a loud noise with angry voices. Frightened and hastily trying to dress, she could hear hurried steps running up the staircase. His loud voice was saying, "You cannot go up there." As she looked up, standing in the doorway, was a very attractive, very pregnant woman with blood in her eyes. With the murderous look on her face, long, dangerous-looking, dangling fingernails. Without warning, she sprang on Susan like a wildcat, wrapping her dangerous nails around her neck, digging into her soft flesh. She threw her to the floor, punching her all over, overpowering her, being a much bigger person. Never before had she been so embarrassed. Lying on the floor, half-naked, fighting for her life, grabbing her hair, pulling as hard as she could, causing painful screams.

James, with much difficulty, was able to separate them. Susan's skin burned from painful scratches all over her body. She wondered, *How did I get into this mess?* James had a hard time controlling the stranger as she wrestled like a wildcat, scratching him as well. He yelled out, "Stop it," as he pinned her down in a chair, trying to get her to calm down, but she continued to scream and yell, asking him what she had done to deserve this unfaithfulness. She accused him of being a cheater and bringing another woman into their bed.

Shamed with embarrassment, he packed a small bag and left without saying a word. He left Susan and the stranger behind. After calming down, the stranger introduced herself as Margaret and apologized after she explained her story and how much she was lied to, not knowing he lived with someone. Susan and Margaret had a civil conversation and exchanged numbers before parting company. This was her first and last experience fighting with another woman. She went back to her old way of life, which was a much more savory and simpler way to live, wanting to reach to a ripe old age.

Her friend Faye was also in a hot mess when her lover's wife came home. He stopped paying her bills, forcing her to move into the arms of another man with the same MO. I asked her why. Her passive answer was "It's life. You lose some, and you win some. Life is a gamble."

Dating a married man is a risk. You just have to make the right pick. Married men are the best providers. Married or not, they are all mostly cheaters. There is only a 10 percent faithfulness rate, according to Faye. This she will always remember, along with her souvenir scars.

About the Author

Nader Somoye is an inspiring new writer from the lovely Caribbean island of Jamaica, West Indies. Her love of the great outdoors, nature, and interacting with people inspired her passion for writing at a tender age. Lately, she has developed a more pressing desire to write real stories based on her life's journeys. She hopes her stories will bring you laughter and make an impact on your life.

Printed in the United States
By Bookmasters